Our

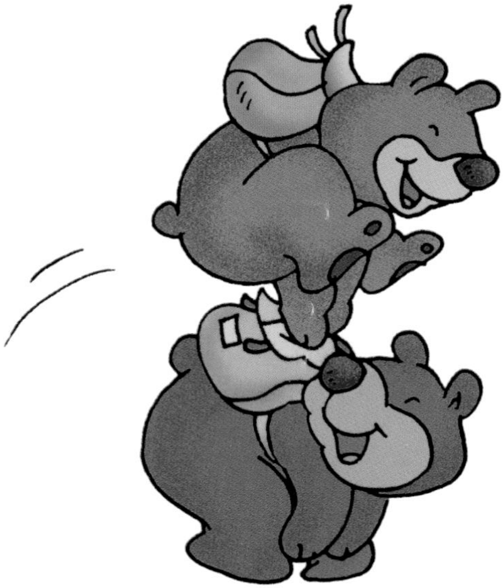

Illustrated by Stella Yang

Rigby

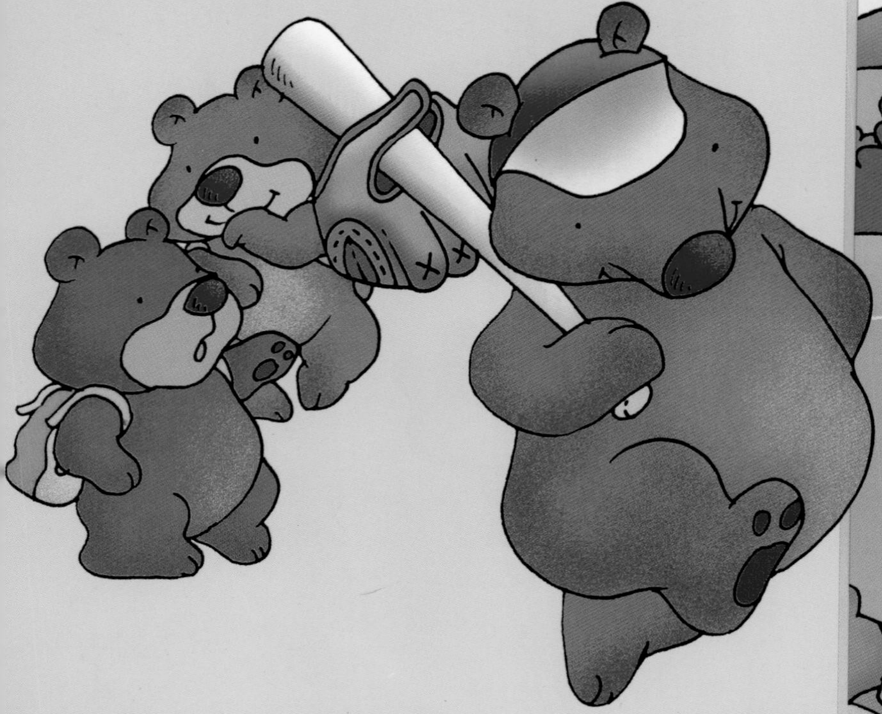

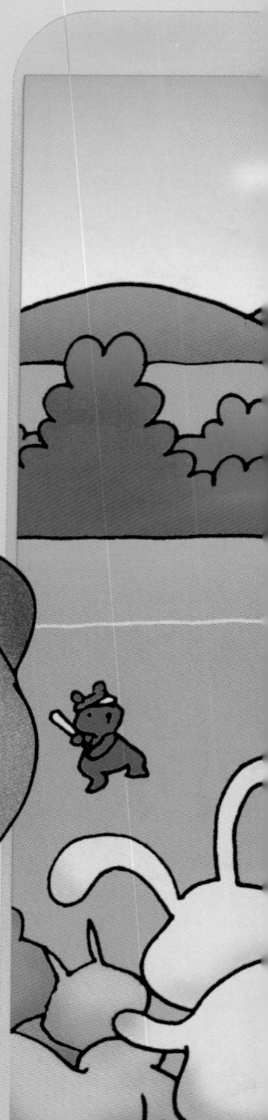

We went
to the game.

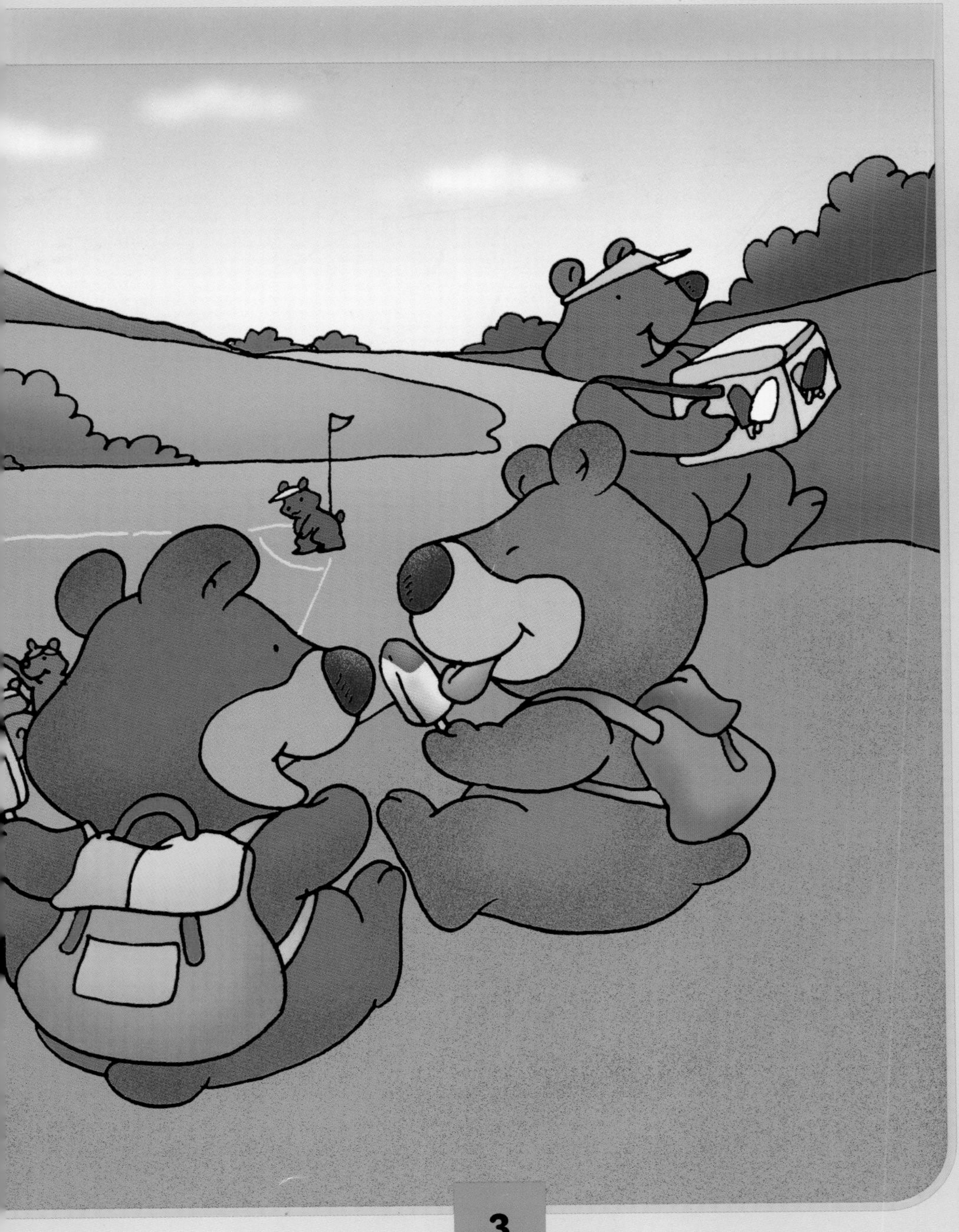

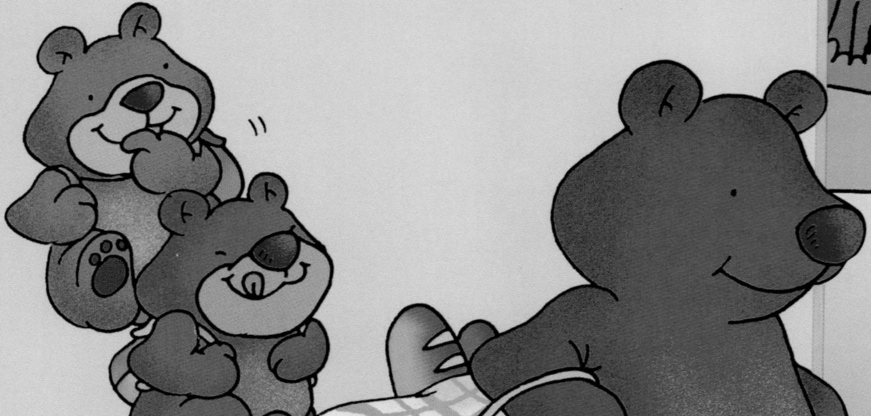
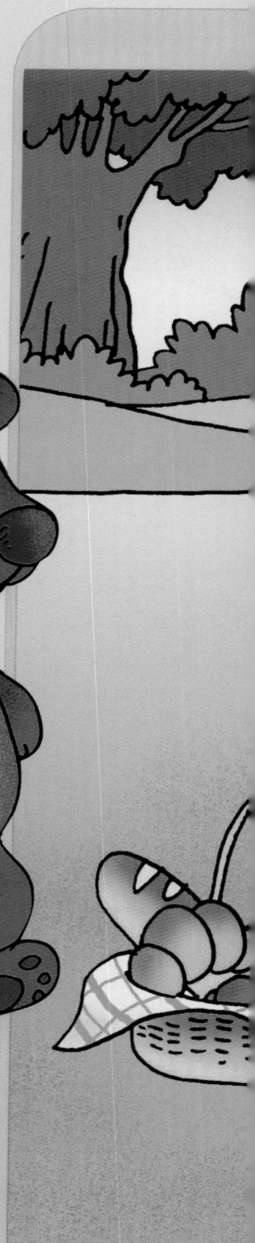

We went
to the picnic.

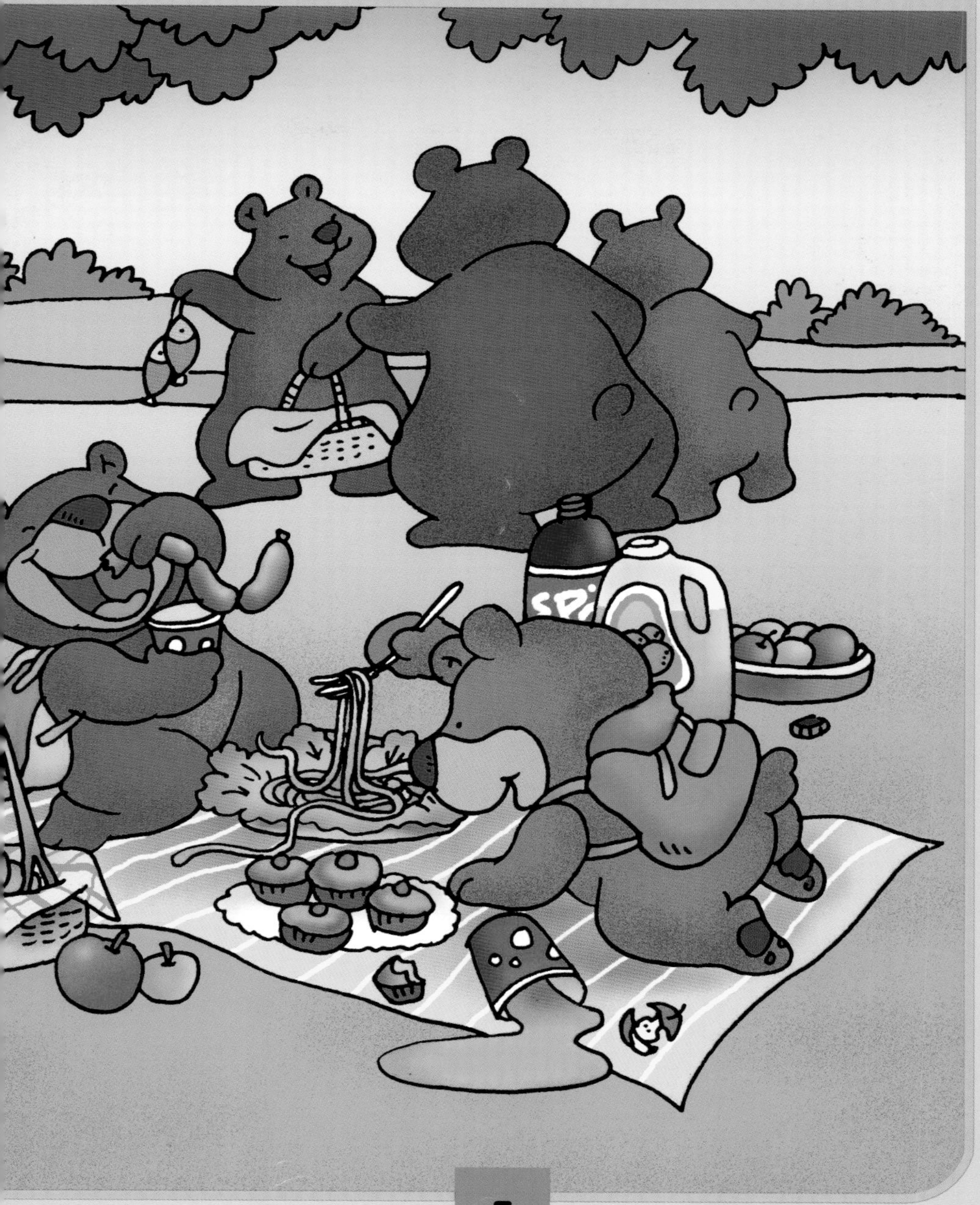

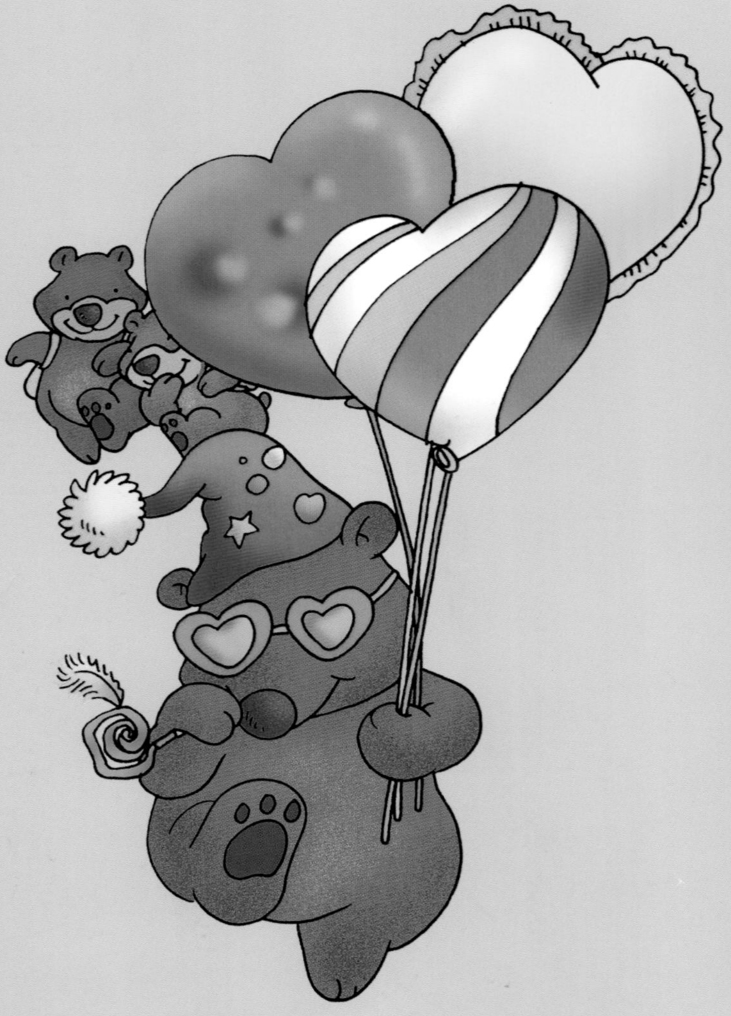

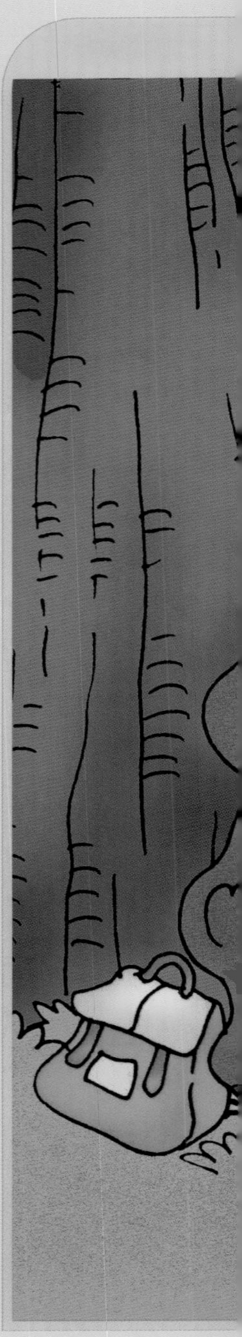

We went
to the party.

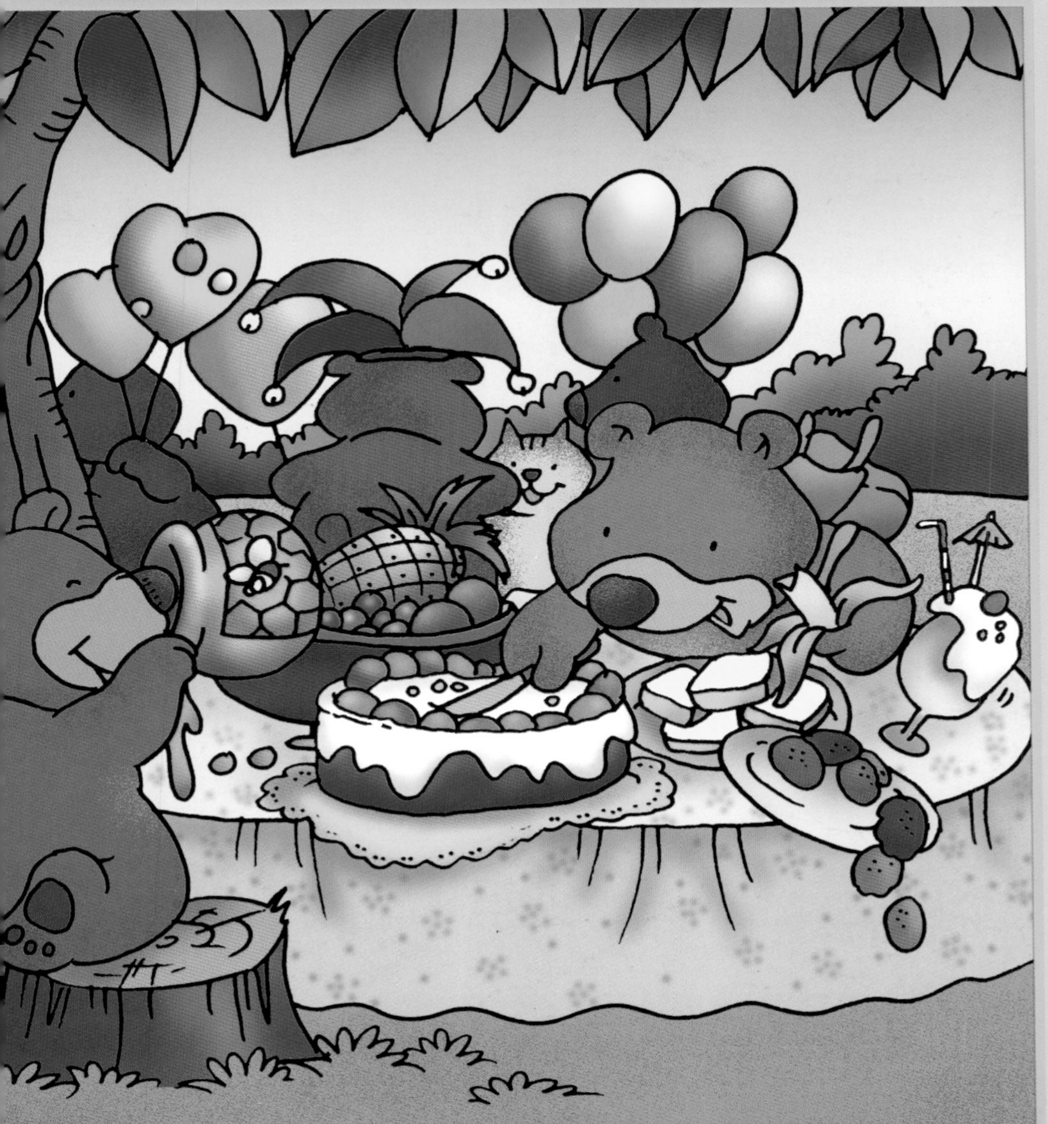

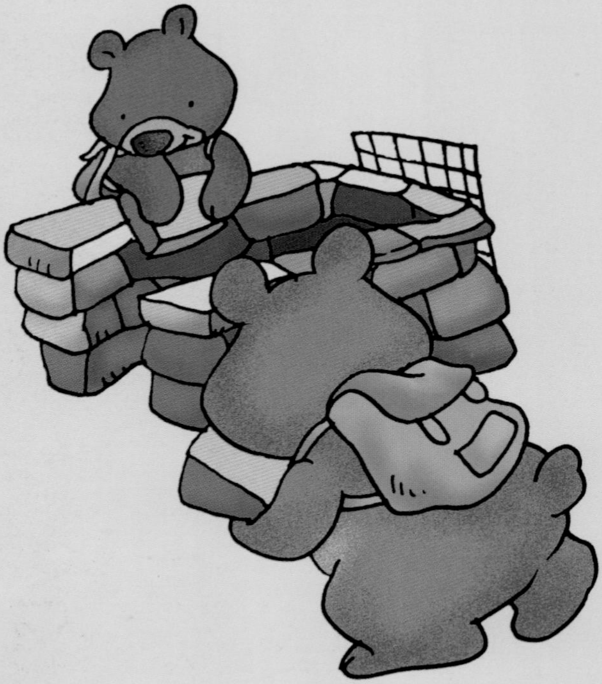

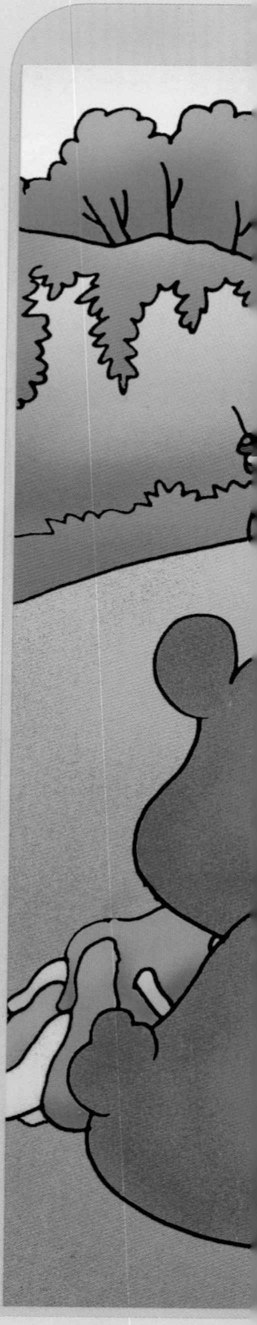

We went
to the barbecue.

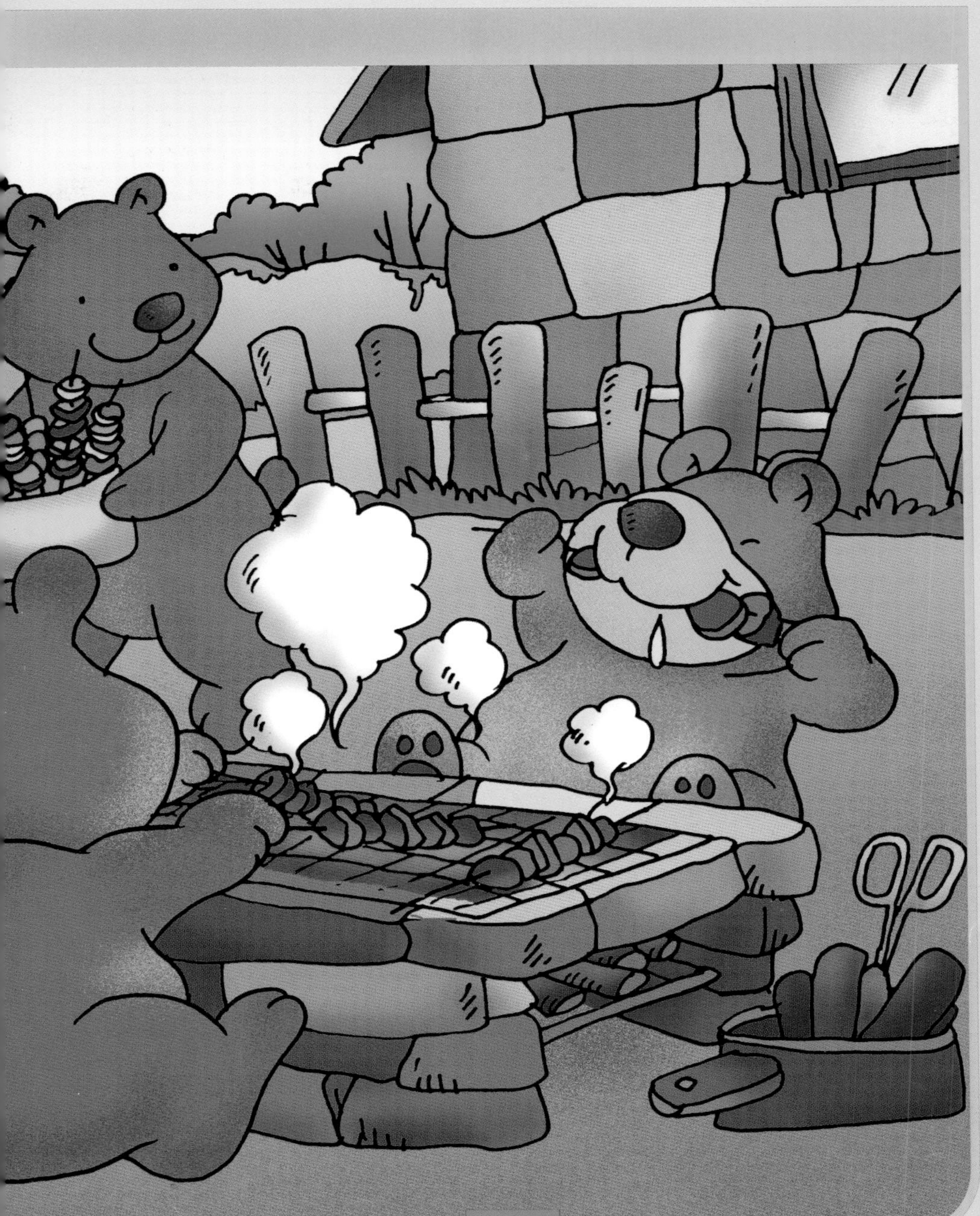

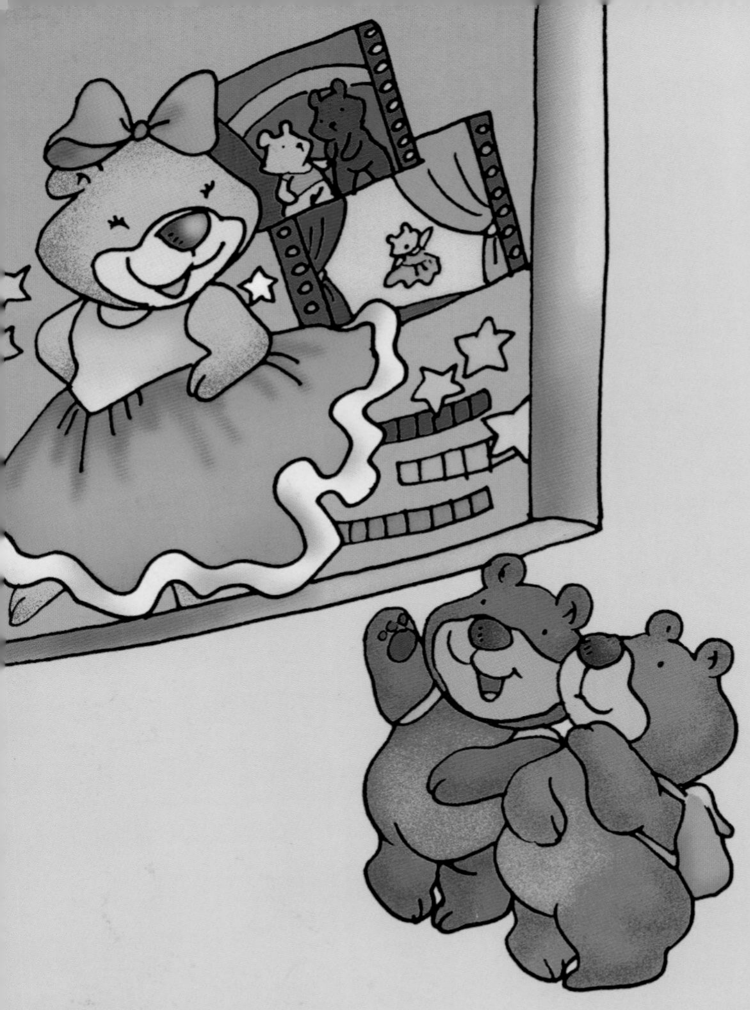

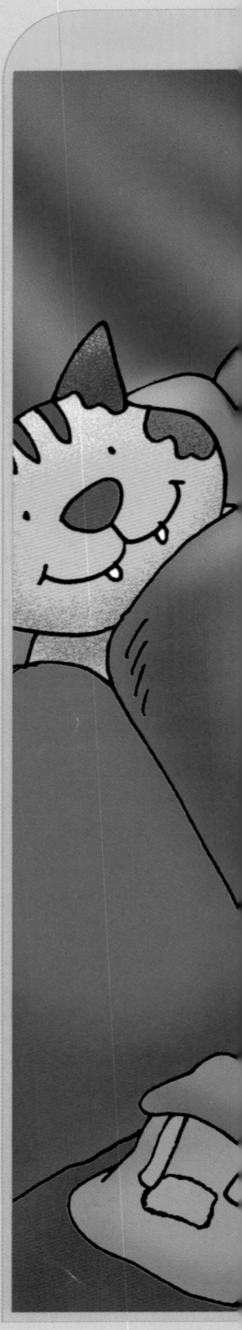

We went
to the movies.

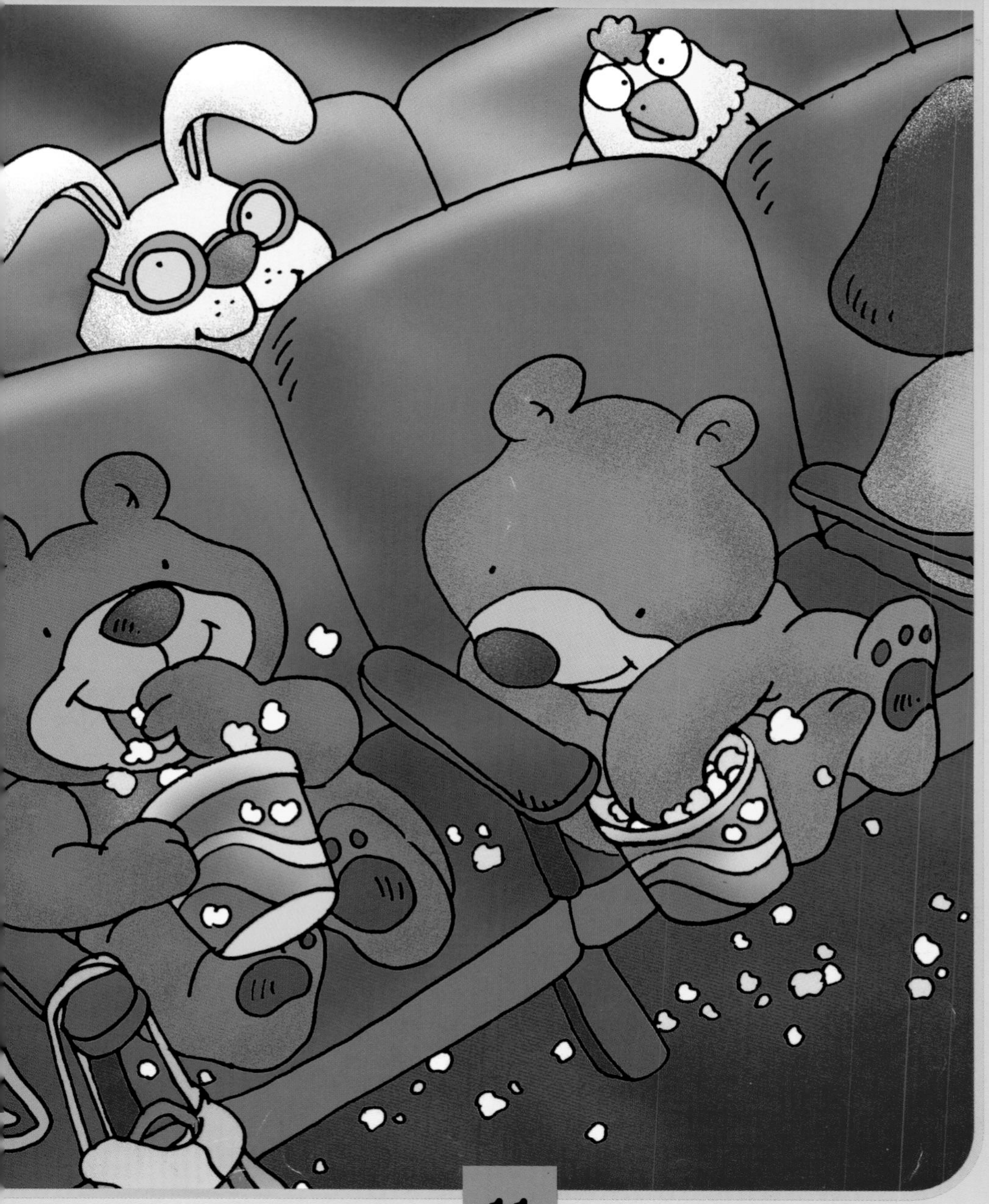

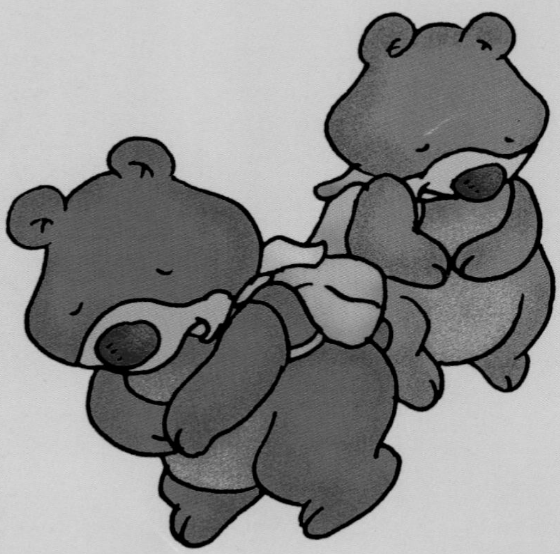

We went
to the doctor.

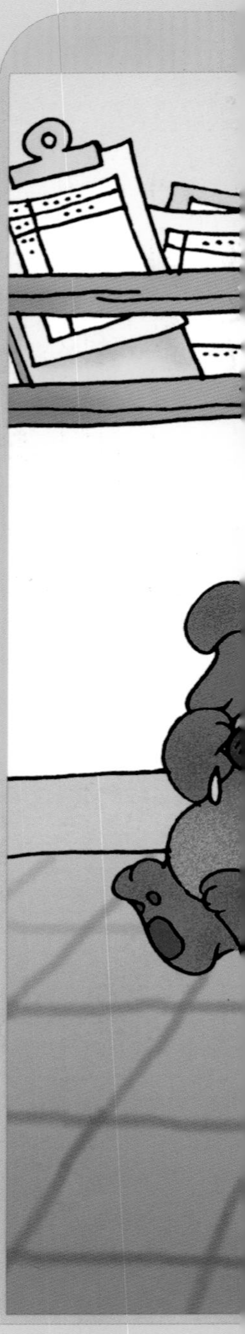

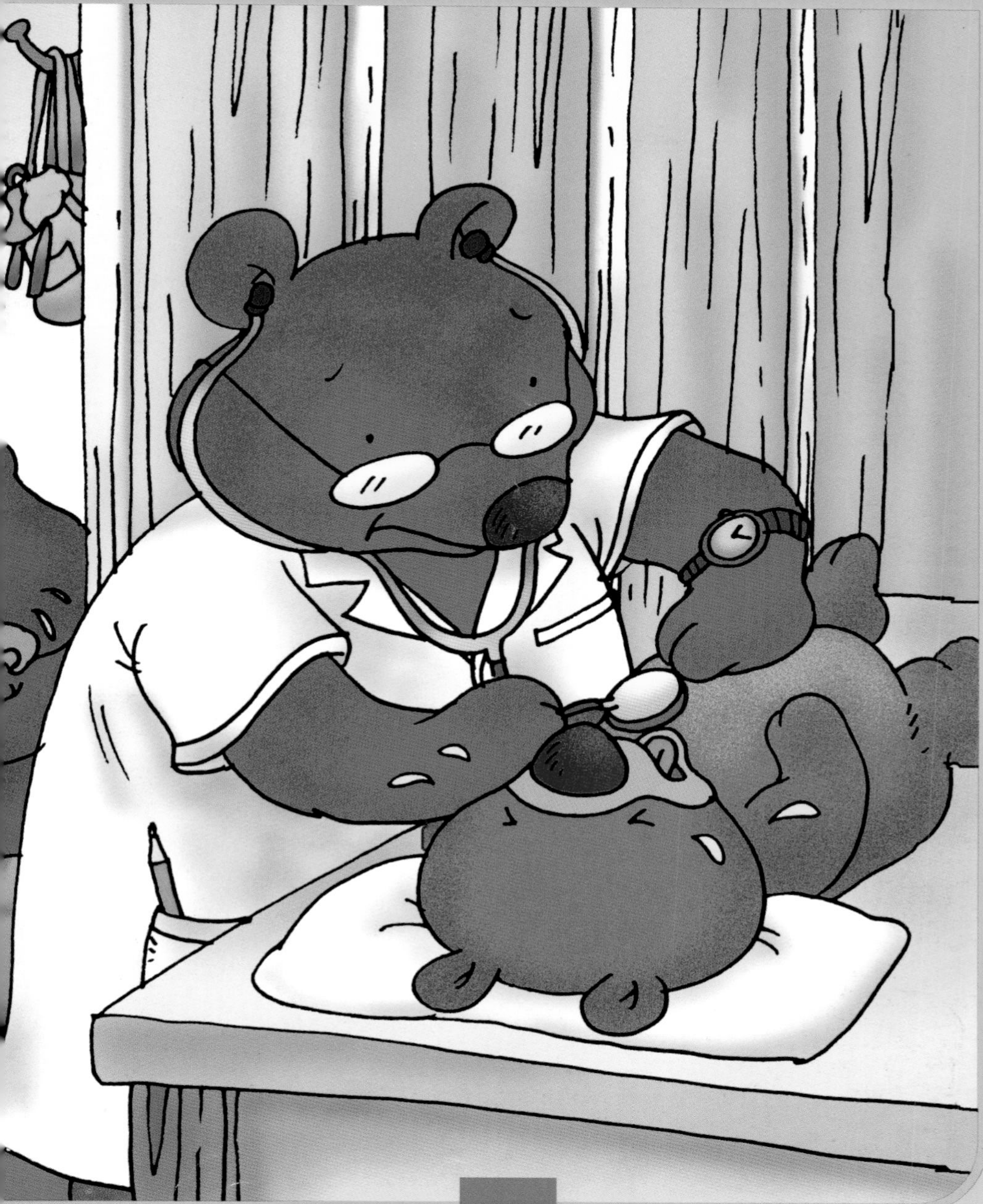

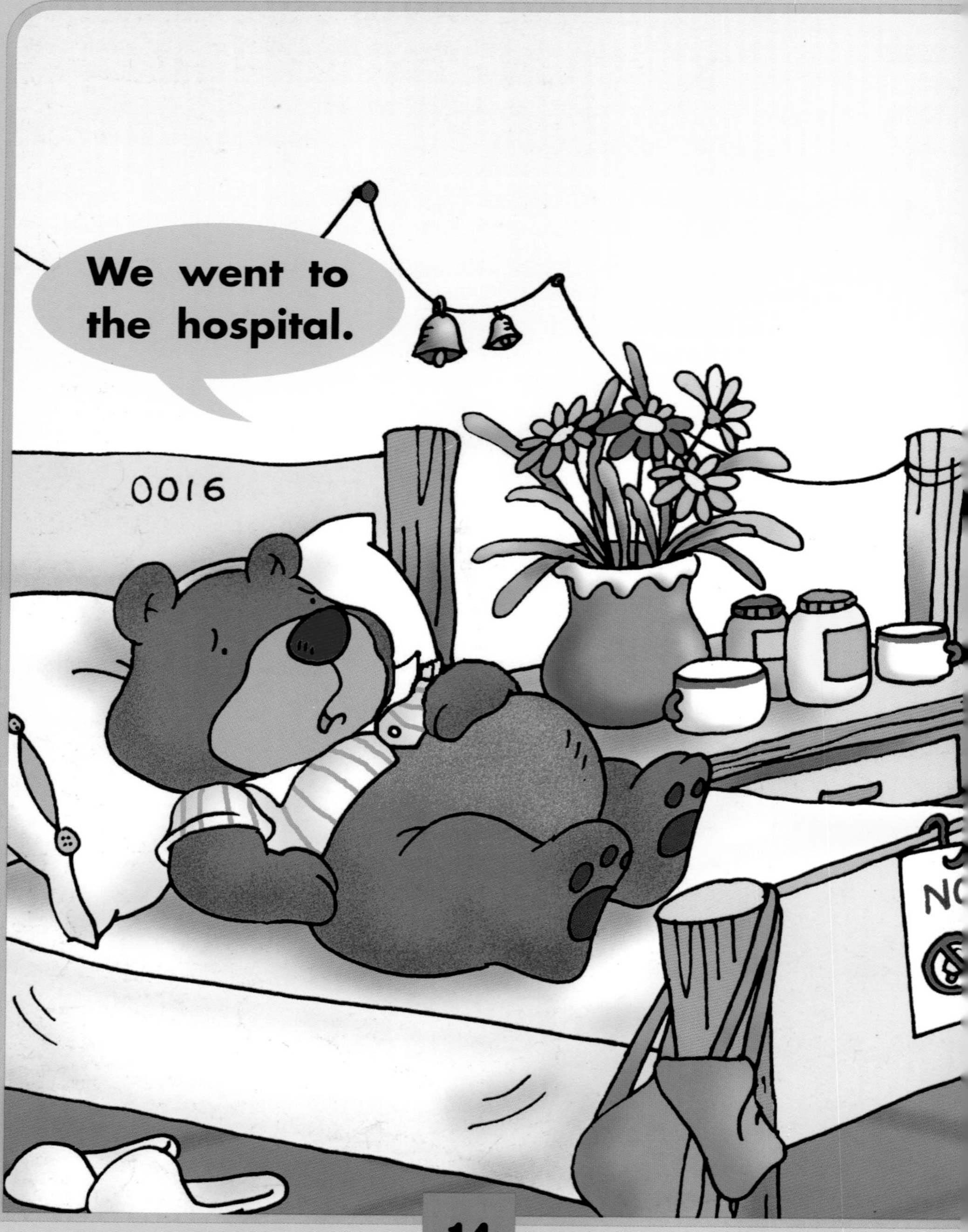
We went to the hospital.
0016

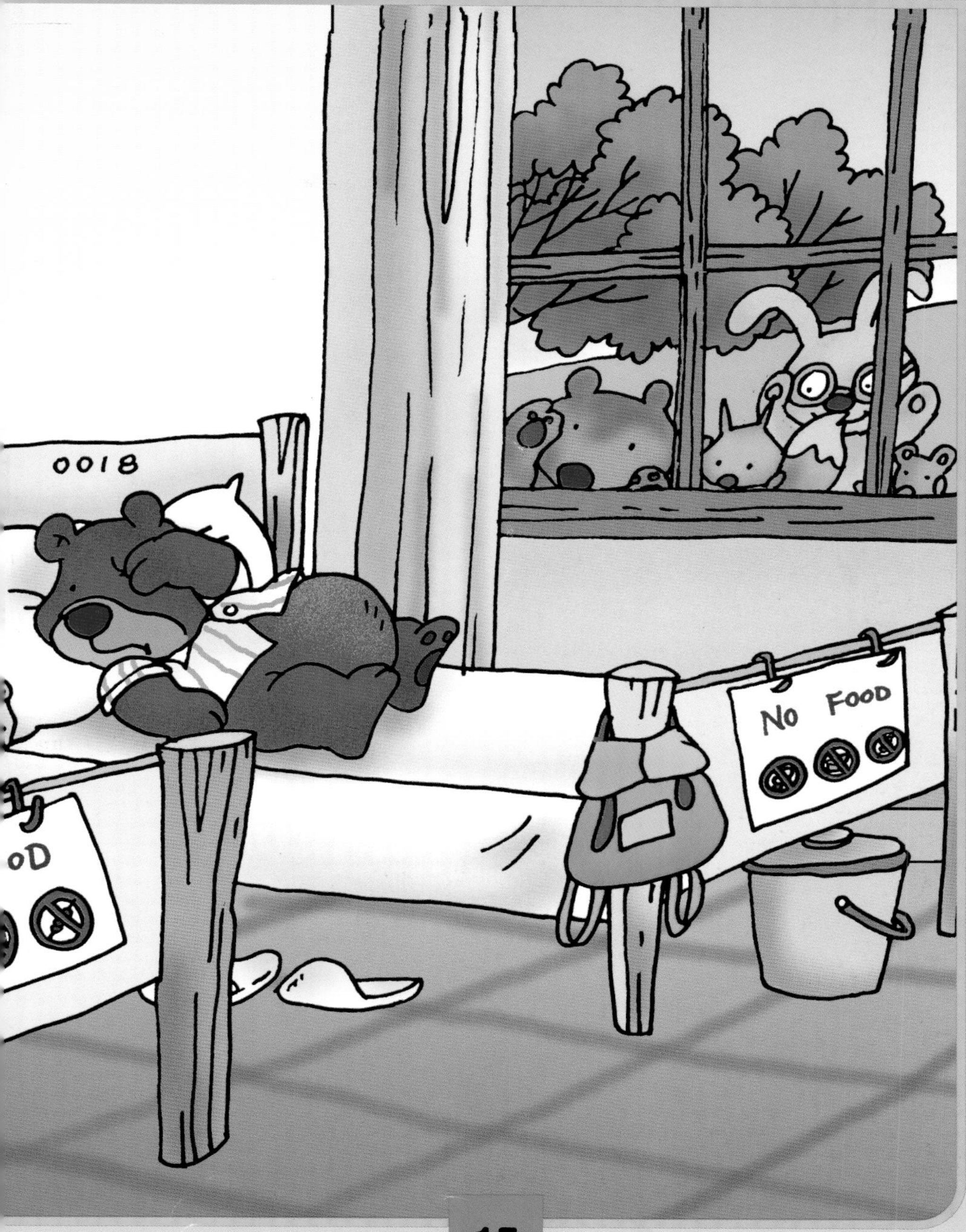
0018
No Food
oD

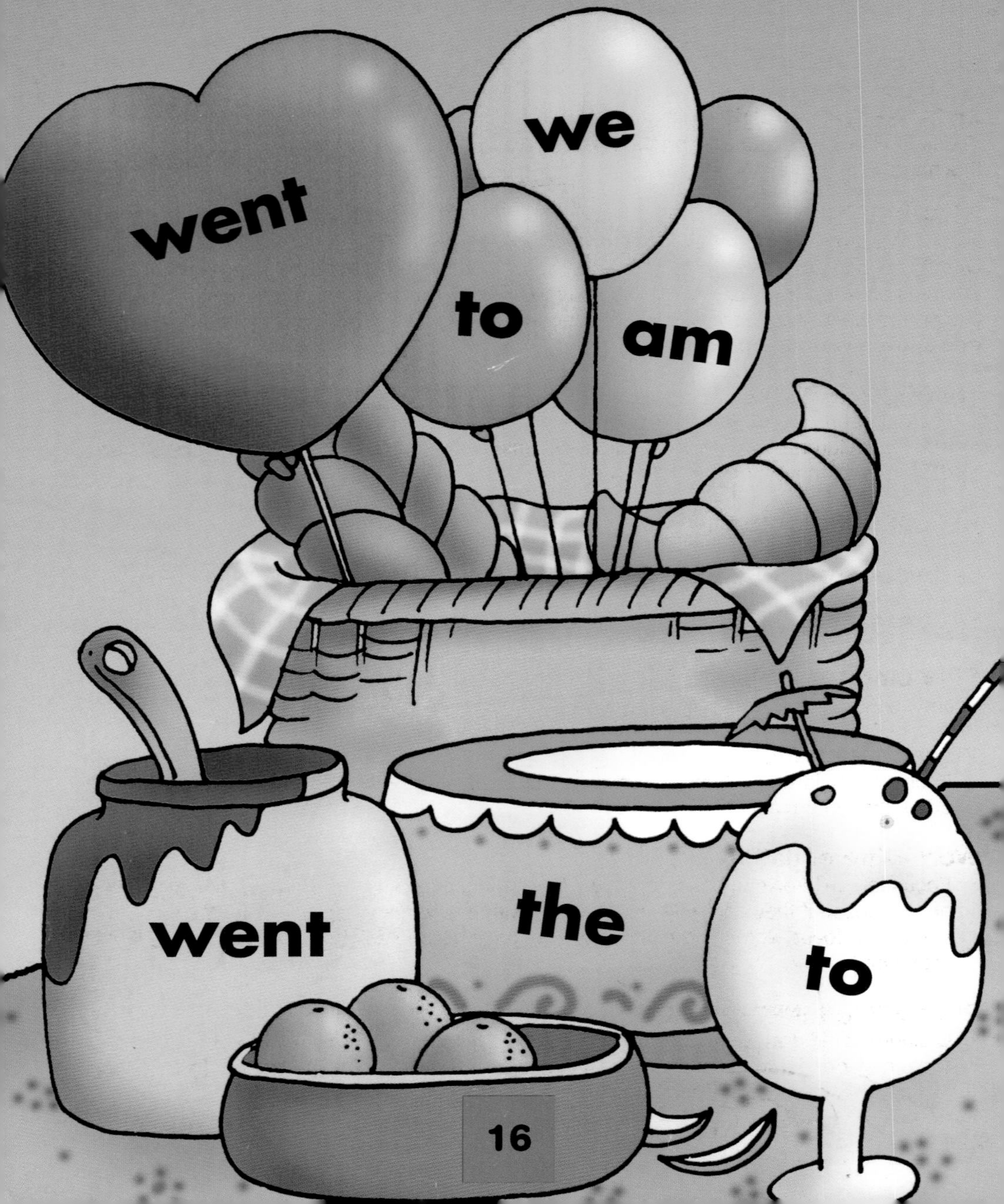
went
we
to
am
went
the
to